Table · Chair · Bear

Table · Chair · Bear

A BOOK IN MANY LANGUAGES

by Jane Feder

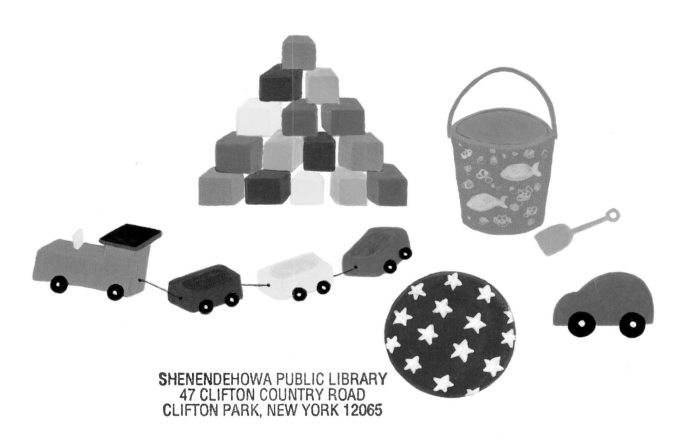

TICKNOR & FIELDS BOOKS FOR YOUNG READERS

NEW YORK 1995

The author wishes to acknowledge Berlitz Translation Services for translations and phonetic spellings, Dora Johnson and the Center for Applied Linguistics for guidance in the selection of languages, Judy Levin for editorial assistance, and David Saylor for encouragement in the preparation of the art.

Published by Ticknor & Fields Books for Young Readers,
A Houghton Mifflin company, 215 Park Avenue South,
New York, New York 10003.

Manufactured in the United States of America
Book design by Sylvia Frezzolini Severance
The illustrations are acrylic paintings, reproduced in full color

WOZ 10 9 8 7 6 5 4 3 2 1

Library of Congress Cataloging-in-Publication Data
Feder, Jane.
Table, chair, bear : a book in many languages / by Jane Feder.
p. cm.
Summary: Presents illustrations of objects found in a child's room, labeled in
thirteen different languages, including Spanish, Vietnamese, Japanese, and French.
ISBN 0-395-65938-8
[1. Polyglot materials. 2. Vocabulary.]
PZ10.5.F44Tab 1995
413'.21—dc20 92-40529 CIP AC

Thanks to Norma Jean!

Author's Note

Never before have so many languages been spoken in this country as can be heard today. Including every one of them in this book was not possible. Most of the languages here—Korean, French, Arabic, Vietnamese, Japanese, Portuguese, Lao, Spanish, Chinese, Tagalog, and Cambodian—are being spoken by more and more children, many of them new to the United States. Navajo, a language spoken on this continent before English, is included because it is the Native American language with the most speakers.

This book is for children who speak any of these languages. For children who are curious about languages other than their own, phonetic spellings have been included. A few symbols used in the phonetic spellings may not be familiar, and the guide below will help with their pronunciation. Some of the pronunciations have been simplified for young readers, but they are still very close to the authentic sounds of the languages.

PHONETIC SYMBOL	SOUND
aa	calm (like the *a* in father, but longer)
kh	yech (We do not often use this sound in English, but we do when we say, "Yech! That's disgusting!")
lh	This sounds a little like an *s*. Put your tongue as you would to make an *l*, but instead of making the *l*, blow air around your tongue. (This sound is not used in English.)
uh	book
zh	garage
ə	item, about
'	This stands for a little stop made in the the back of the throat, like the one in the middle of "Uh-oh!"
?	This tells us to raise our voice, as we do when asking a question. (In Chinese and Vietnamese, raising the voice in this way changes the meaning of the word.)
‿	Two letters marked this way are run together, as they are in boil.

The languages appear in this order:

English

Korean

French

Arabic

Vietnamese

Japanese

Portuguese (Brazilian)

Lao

Spanish (Mexican)

Chinese (Mandarin)

Tagalog

Cambodian

Navajo

아기 곰
ah-kee-KOM

un ours en peluche
uhn oors ah peh-loosh

دب
dib

con gấu
KONG gah-oo?

くま
KOO-mah

um ursinho
de pelúcia
oom oor-SEEN-yoh duh puh-LOO-see-ah

ໝີ
mee?

un osito
oon oh-SEE-toh

玩具熊
wan jee-YOO SHEE-oong

laruang oso
lah-roo-AHNG OH-soh

ຂາຍຄຳ
KLAAR-kmohm

daane'é shash
dah-NEH-eh shəsh

bear

behr

chair

chehr

의자
OO‐EE-jah

une chaise
oon shehz

كرسي
KUHR-see

ghế
geh?

いす
ee-SOO

uma cadeira
OO-mah kah-DAY-rah

ເກົ້າອີ້
tang-EE

una sillita
OO-nah see-YEE-tah

椅子
EE dzuh

silya
SEEL-yah

ເກົ້າອີ້
KOW‐ai

bikáá' dah'asdáhí
bə-KAA dah-hahs-DAH-hah

mirror

MIR-ər

거울
KOH-wool

un miroir
uh meer-wahr

مرآة
meer-AAT

gương
goo-ung

かがみ
kah-GAH-mee

um espelho
oom ehs-PEH-lee‿oh

ກະຈົກເງົາ
gah-CHOK-now

un espejo
oon ehs-PEH-hoh

镜子
JEENG dzuh

salamin
sah-lah-MEEN

កញ្ចក់
KAHN-chah

bii'adeest'įį
BEE-ə-DEHS-t'hing

tricycle

TRAI-si-kəl

자전거
CHAH-chun-koh

un tricycle
uh tree-see-klə

دراجة
duhr-RAH-zhuh

xe đạp ba bánh
seh DAP ba ban?

さんりんしゃ
san-lin-SHAH

um triciclo
oom tree-SEE-kloh

ຣົດສາມລໍ້
loht-sam-LAH

un triciclo
oon tree-SEE-kloh

三轮脚踏车
SAN LOO-ehn jee‿YOW TAH chuh

traysikel
TRAI-see-kel

ក្ង៓ទកង៝
kow‿ung-KAHNG

dzi'izi bijááad t'á'igíí
tsi-ZI-i bə-JAAD T'AH-ah-gee

창 문
CHAHNG-moon

une fenêtre
oon fuh-neh-trə

نافذة
NAA-fee-zuh

cửa sổ
koo-wah? shoh?

まど
MAH-doh

uma janela
OO-mah zhah-NEH-lah

ບ່ອງຫ້ຽມ
pong-EE˰əm

una ventana
OO-nah vehn-TAH-nah

窗户
CHWONG hoo

bintana
bin-TAH-nah

បង្អួច
BOHNG-oo˰i

tsézǫ́
TSEH-sohng

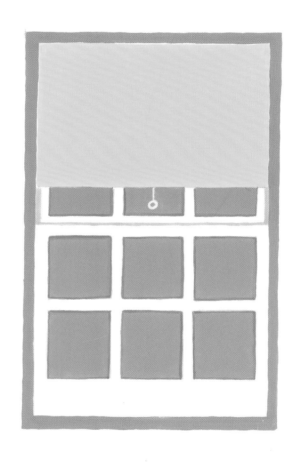

easel

EE-zəl

이젤
EE-jehl

un chevalet
uh shuh-vah-lay

حامل
HAA-mel

giá vẽ
yah? veh⌣yah?

イーゼル
EE-zehl

um cavalete
oom kah-vah-LEH-teh

ม้าตั้งรูป
maa-TANG-hoop

un caballete
oon kah-bah-YEH-teh

画板架
HWAH ba⌣an jee⌣AH

kabalyete
kah-bah-LYEH-teh

ជើងជ្រ
CHEE⌣oong-troh

bikáá' na'a'ch'ąąhí dah sitánígíí
bə-KAA nah-ah-CH'AH-hah dah sə-TAH-ni-gee

그림
KOO-reem

des images
dayz eem-ahzh

صور
SOO-wahr

hình vẽ
HENN veh‿yah?

え
eh

uns desenhos
oons deh-ZEHN-yohs

รูป
hoop

unas pinturas
OO-nahs peen-TOO-rahs

图画
too? HWAH

mga larawan
mahng-AH lah-RAH-wahn

រូបភាព
roo-PEE‿yup

naałtsoos bikáá' e'elaaígíí
NAHLH-tsohs bə-KAA eh-ehl-YAH-i-gee

pictures

PIK-chərz

table
TAY-bəl

테이블
TAY-bəl

une table
oon tah-blə

طاولة
TAA-wi-luh

bàn
baan

テーブル
TAY-buh-loo

uma mesa
OO-mah MEH-zah

โต๊ะ
toh

una mesa
OO-nah MEH-sah

桌子
joo‿OH dzuh

lamesa
lah-MEH-sah

តុ
tok

bikáá' adáni
bə-KAA ah-DAH-nah

문
moon

une porte
oon pohrt

باب
baab

cửa
koo-wah?

ドア
DOH-ah

uma porta
OO-mah POHR-tah

ប្រទូ
pah-TOO

una puerta
OO-nah poo-EHR-tah

门
mun?

pintuan
pin-TOO-AHN

ទ្វារ
tweer

dáádiłkał
daa-DILH-kalh

door

dawr

doll

dahl

인형
IN-hyong

une poupée
oon poo-pay

دمية
DOO-meh-yuh

búp bê
BUHP beh

にんぎょう
NIN-gyoh

uma boneca
OO-mah boh-NEH-kah

ຕຸ໊ກກະຕາ
TOOK-ga-tah

una muñeca
OO-nah moo-NYEH-kah

洋娃娃
YAHNG? wah? wah

manyika
mahn-YEE-kah

កូនក្រមុំ
kah⌣oon-KROH-məm

áwééshchiin
ah-WAYSH-cheen

라디오
rah-DEE‿oh

une radio
oon rah-dee‿oh

راديو
RAA-dyoh

máy phát thanh
ma-ee? fa? TAN

ラジオ
LAH-zhee‿oh

um rádio
oom HAH-dee‿oh

ວິທະຍຸ
vi-TA-nyuh

una radio
OO-nah RAH-dee‿yoh

收音机
shoh een jee

radyo
RAH-dee‿oh

វិទ្យុ
WI-t'hee‿uh

niłch'i hałne'é
NILH-ch'i halh-NEH-eh

radio
RAY-dee-oh

lamp

lamp

램프
RAM-poo

une lampe
oon lahmp

مصباح
MIS-baah

đèn
dhenn

ランプ
LAN-puh

um abajur
oom ah-bah-ZHOOR

โคมไฟ
kohm-FAI

una lámpara
OO-nah LAHM-pah-rah

台灯
tah‿ee duhng

lampara
LAHM-pəh-rah

ចង្កៀង
chahng-KEE‿UNG

bee'adinídínígíí
beh-ah-DI-ni-DI-ni-gee

toys

장난감
CHAHNG-nan-kahm

des jouets
day zhoo‿eh

لُعَب
LOO-ahb

đồ chơi
DOH choy‿ee

おもちゃ
oh-MOH-chah

uns brinquedos
oons breeng-KYEH-dohs

ເຄື່ອງຫຼິ້ນເດັກນ້ອຍ
kuh‿oong-LIN-dek-NOY

unos juguetes
OO-nohs hoo-GEH-tehs

玩具
wan jee‿YOO

mga laruan
mahng-AH lah-roo‿AHN

ប្រដាប់លេង
broh-DAP-ling

daane'é
dah-NEH-eh

선반
SUN-bahn

une étagère
oon ay-tah-zhehr

رف
rəf

kệ sách
KEH shat?

たな
tah-NAH

uma prateleira
OO-mah prah-teh-LAY-rah

ຊັ້ນຖ້ວຍ
san-TOO

un estante
oon ehs-TAHN-teh

架子
jee-_AH dzuh

istante
is-TAHN-teh

ធ្នើ
t'ung

bikáá' dah ná'a'nilígíí
bə-KAA dah nah-ah-NILH-i-gee

shelf

shehlf

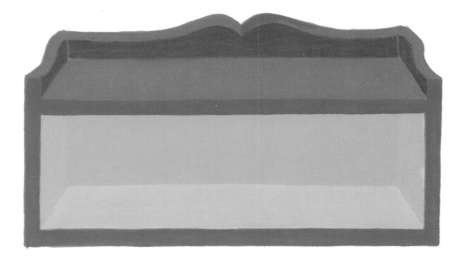

basket

BAS-kit

휴지통
HYOO-jee-tong

une corbeille
à papiers
oon kohr-bay ah pah-pyay

سلة مهملات
SAL-lət MUH-meh-lat

giỏ rác
ZHAH rak?

くずかご
kee͟oo-ZOO KAH-goh

uma cesta
OO-mah SEHS-tah

ກະຕ່າ
ga-TAA

un cesto de basura
oon SEHS-toh deh bah-SOO-rah

桶
tohng

basurahan
BAH-soo-rəh-HAHN

កញ្ច្រែង
KAHNG-chraing

ts'iilzéí bii' ha'nílígíí
t'seel-ZAY bee hah-NILH-i-gee

러그
RAH-goo

un tapis
uh tah-pee

سجادة
soo-JA-duh

tấm thảm
TAM tahm?

じゅうたん
JOO-tan

um tapete
oom tah-PEH-teh

ผ้าปู
POHM-poo

un tapete
oon tah-PEH-teh

小地毯
shee-yow DEE ta‿an

alpombra
ahl-POHM-brah

ព្រំ
proom

ni'góó sikaadígíí
neh-OH sə-KAH-di-gee

rug
rug

bed

behd

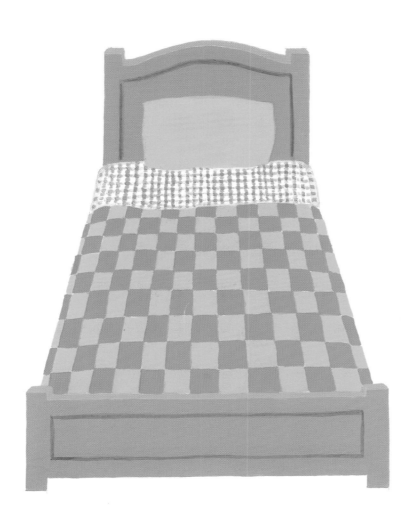

침대
CHEEM-deh

un lit
uh lee

سرير
sa-REER

giường
zoo-ung

ベッド
BEH-ddoh

uma cama
OO-mah KUH-mah

ຕຽງນອນ
tee-eng-NOHN

una cama
OO-nah KAH-mah

牀
CHWONG?

kama
KAH-mah

គ្រែ
kray

tsásk'eh
TSAHS-k'eh

마차
MAA-chah

un chariot
uh shah-ree‿oh

عربة
A-rah-buh

xe kéo
SEH kay‿oh?

ワゴン
WAH-gon

um carrinho
oom kah-HEENG-yoh

ริกลาก
loht-LAAK

un carrito
oon kahr-REE-toh

玩具手拉车
wan jee‿YOO shoh‿oo LAH chuh

kariton
kah-ree-TOHN

កូនម្ជារនអូស
kow‿ung-LAAN-ohs

tsinááḅąąs yazhi
tsin-aa-BAHS YAH-zhah

wagon
WAG-gən

clock

klahk

시계
SHEE-keh

un réveil
uh reh-vey

ساعة
SAA-uh

đồng hồ để bàn
DONG HOH day? BAAN

とけい
toh-kay‿EE

um relógio
oom heh-LAW-zhoh

มาริกา
NAH-ree-KAA

un reloj
oon reh-LOHKH

钟
johng

orasan
oh-rah-SAHN

ธាឡ្យិការរោ
NEER-leh-kaa-roh

na'oolkiłi
nah-ohl-KILH-eh

옷장
OHT-chahng

une commode
oon koh-mohd

خزانة
khi-ZAH-nuh

tủ áo
tah⌣oo? ow?

たんす
TAN-suh

uma cômoda
OO-mah KOH-moh-dah

ຕູ້ໃສ່ເຄື່ອງນຸ່ງ
TOO-sai-KUH⌣OONG-noong

una cómoda
OON-nah KOH-moh-dah

五斗柜
oo? doh⌣oo GWAY

kabinet
KAH-bee-net

ប័ត្ទូ
T'AA-t'oo

ée' bii ná'niłi
eh bee nah-NILH-eh

books

buhks

책
chek

des livres
day lee-vrə

kuh-TUB

sách vở
SHAT vah‿uh?

ほん
hon

uns livros
oons LEE-vrohs

ປຶ້ມ
puh‿oom

unos libros
OO-nos LEE-bros

书
shoo

mga aklat
mahng-AH ahk-LAHT

សៀវភៅ
see‿oo-PUH‿OH

naaltsos wolta'ígíí
NAHLH-tsohs wolh-TAH-i-gee

my room

mai room

내 방
nay-BAHNG

ma chambre
mah shahm-brə

غرفتي
GHUR-fah-tee

phòng của tôi
FOM koo-wah? TOY

わたしのへや
wah-tah-SHEE noh hay-YAH

meu quarto
MEH‿oh KWAHR-toh

ຫ້ອງຂອງຂ້ອຍ
HONG-kong-KOY

mi recámara
mee reh-KAH-mah-rah

我的房间
WAW‿uh duh FONG jee‿EHN

ang aking silid
ahng ah-KING see-LID

បន្ទប់ខ្ញុំ
bun-TOP-knyohm

sitsáske tsi'ání góne'
shə-TSAHS-k'eh tsə'-AH-nah GOH-neh

들어오세요
TOO-roh-OH-seh‿YOH

Please come in

pleez kum in

Entrez
ah-tray

تفضل
təf-FAH-DDAL

Xin mời vào
sin moy‿ee vow

どうぞはいってください。
DOH-zoh HAI-tteh-koo-dah-SA‿EE

Entre por favor
EHN-treh pohr fah-VOHR

ខើ្ញខ៊ាមា
sern-KOW-mah?

Por favor pase
pohr fah-VOHR PAH-seh

请进来
cheeng JIN lah‿ee

Tuloy po kayo
too-LOY POH kah‿YOH

សូមអញ្ជើញចូលក្នុង
SOHM-ang-chee‿ung-jee‿ohl-KNONG

Wósh déę́ yah aninááh
WUHSH day yah AH-neh-naa